King Jack
and the
Dragon

For Theo, alias King Jack, and his den-building friends — P.B.

For Jesse — H.O.

PUFFIN BOOKS

Published by the Penguin Group: London, New York, Australia,
Canada, India, Ireland, New Zealand and South Africa
Penguin Books Ltd, Registered Offices: 80 Strand, London WC2R ORL, England

puffinbooks.com

First published 2011
001 – 10 9 8 7 6 5 4 3 2 1

Text copyright © Peter Bently, 2011
Illustrations copyright © Helen Oxenbury, 2011

Made and printed in China
ISBN: 978-0-141-32759-4

King Jack
and the
Dragon

PETER BENTLY & HELEN OXENBURY

PUFFIN

Jack, Zak and Caspar
were making a den,
a mighty great fort for King Jack and his men.

A big cardboard box,

an old sheet and some sticks,

a couple of bin bags,
a few broken bricks.

A fine royal throne
from a ragged old quilt,

a drawbridge,

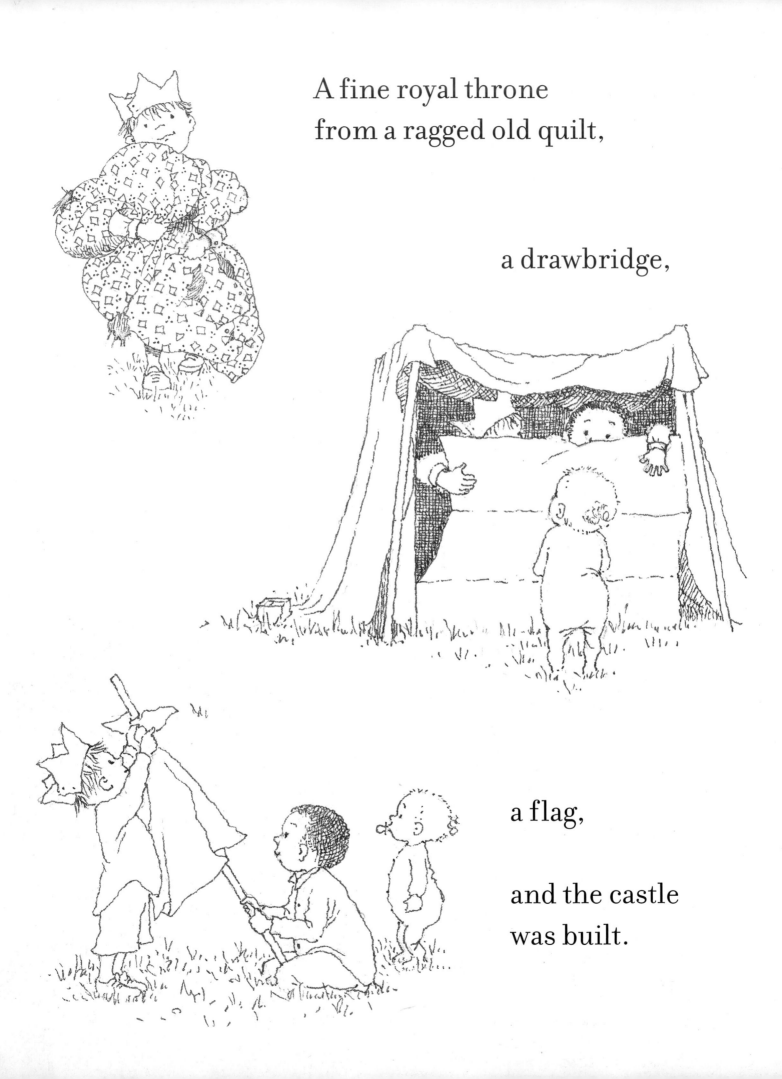

a flag,

and the castle
was built.

"Prepare to do battle, brave knights!"
cried King Jack.
"Protect your king's castle
from dragon attack!"

They spent the whole day . . .

fighting dragons . . .

and beasts . . .

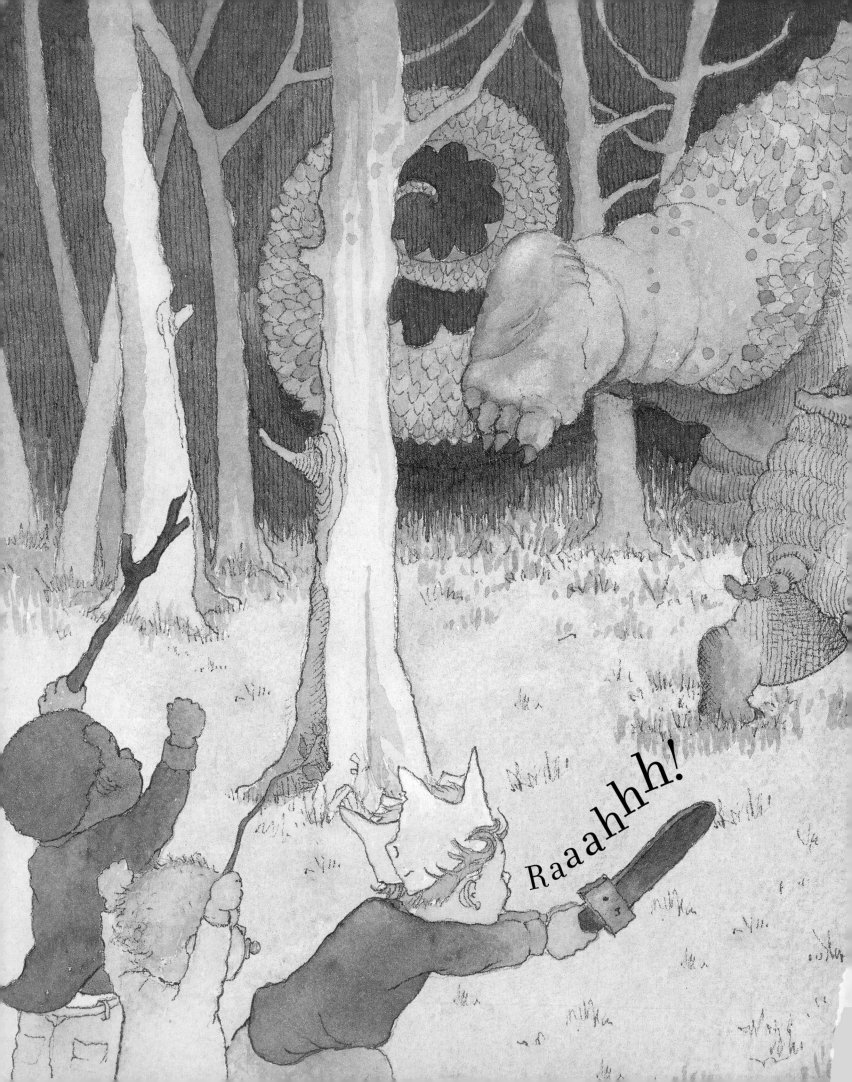

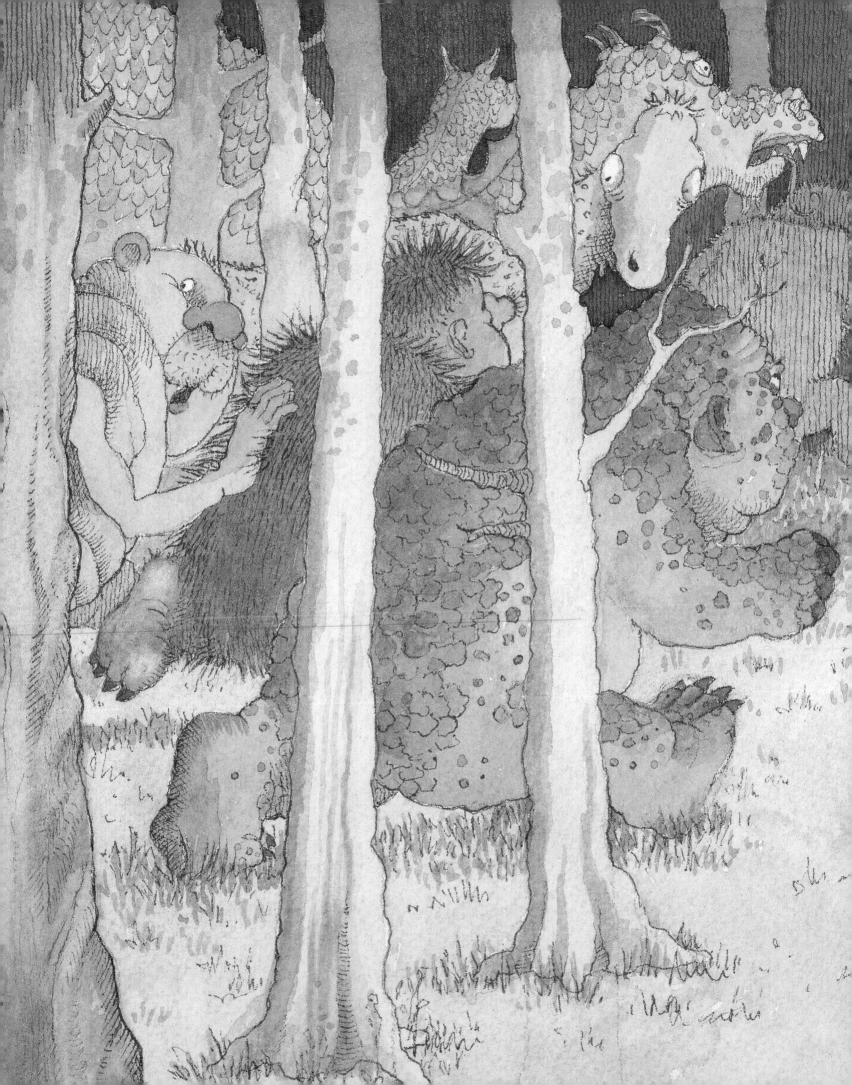

. . . and returned to their stronghold
for fabulous feasts.
"We'll all sleep the night
in the fort," said King Jack.

Then a giant came by
and went home
with Sir Zak.

"Two can fight dragons,
no problem," Jack said . . .

Then another giant came
and took Caspar to bed.

Wrapped up in his blanket,
    Jack sat on his throne.
"All right then," he said. "I'll fight dragons alone."

Then a strong gust of wind
    made the trees start to quiver.
"It's nothing," thought Jack, with a hint of a shiver.

A mouse scampered over the roof,
skitter-scurry.
"It's nothing!" thought Jack.
"There's no reason to worry."

"BRRUP!" croaked a frog.
"It's nothing!" thought Jack,
as he switched on his torch in the deepening black.

"ToO-WhoO!" called an owl. "It's nothing!" Jack said,
as he pulled up his blanket right over his head.

Then
suddenly
brave King Jack's heart
skipped a beat.

He could hear something coming —

a THING
with four feet!

It was outside the drawbridge.

King Jack gave a yelp,

"A dragon! A dragon!

Mum! Dad! Help!"

He wished he was anything else but a king,
as the drawbridge fell open and there stood . . .

the THING!

"We're sorry," smiled Mum, "if we gave you a fright.
　　But it's time for brave kings to come in for the night."
"And kings who've fought dragons all day
　　　need a bath,"
said Dad, as he lifted King Jack
　　　off the path.

"I knew you weren't really a dragon,"
yawned Jack,
as he bravely rode home on a big giant's back.